TO US

Visit us on the Web! www.randomhouse.com/kids

Educators and librarians, for a variety of teaching tools,
visit us at www.randomhouse.com/teachers

www.uglydollbooks.com

Library of Congress Cataloging-in-Publication Data
Horvath, David.
The ugly guide to things that go and things that should go but don't /
by David Horvath and Sun-Min Kim.—1st ed.
p.   cm.
ISBN 978-0-375-84370-9 (trade)
ISBN 978-0-375-93684-5 (lib. bdg.)
I. Kim, Sun-Min.   II. Title.
PZ7.H79222Ugt 2008 [E]—dc22   2007043614

PRINTED IN SINGAPORE
10 9 8 7 6 5 4 3 2 1 First Edition

WAGE

BABO

JEERO

ICE-BAT

WEDGEHEAD

OX

UGLYDOG

MOXY

PEACO

UGLYDOG

TARGET

TRAY

DEER
UGLY

GATO
DELUXE

ABIMA

BIG
TOE

UGLYWORM

POE

UGLY GHOST

PLUNKO

BABO'S BIRD

PUGLEE

CHUCKANUCKA

CINKO

ROAD TRIP!

What do the Uglys do when the pressure of everyday life gets out of control? They eat donuts! And when that doesn't work, they hit the road . . . hard!

ROAD?

TRIP?

The Uglyverse is jam-packed with busy office buildings, crowded streets, and enough shops to put you in the poorhouse! (If you were to shop at each one, that is.) Well, between those overcrowded bundles of city life you'll find miles and miles of road! Freeways, dirt roads, and, of course, dead ends! What to do with all of that pavement? Drive on it! Ride your bike on it! Go sailing on it! That's right, sailing! We'll explain later.

Please do!

ROAD TRIP MUST-HAVES

COMPASS GUIDEBOOK ROAD MAP

DONUT PLATTER ENERGY BAR ENERGY DRINK

If you're going to take a road trip through the Uglyverse, you're going to want some supplies. Sure, you can pack the usual . . . screaming baby, flat tire, and some annoying songs. But be sure to bring lots of snacks and important safety items, such as more snacks.

So off we go! Get your driver's license ready!

WAIT, BUT I DON'T HAVE A DRIVER'S LICENSE!

Beep Beep

DUV

DEPARTMENT OF UGLY VEHICLES

OH BOY.

Before you start crashing into things left and right, you're going to need a driver's license. The only way to get one is to stand in line for a few days.

Don't worry! You'll get a chance to fail the driver's exam once you come back on the third or fourth day. It's a very short wait compared to the one at the Ugly Bank. Convenient, right?

The key to standing in line is to wait all day. The good news is you're not alone! You have hundreds of people in front of you to talk to!

DRIVER'S TEST!

STOP

This means...
- ☐ GO FASTER!
- ☑ SLOW to a Crawl.

YELLOW MEANS...
- ☐ Hold on to your hat!
- ☑ Go! Go! Go!

when your tire is Flat...
- ☑ TIME For a new CAR.
- ☑ GET USED TO WALKING!

Parking Ticket 4 $U

when you get one of these, you...
- ☑ hide it in the glove box.
- ☑ PUT IT ON ANOTHER CAR!

When you take your driver's test, you will endure both the multiple-choice exam and the driving course. Flat cones mean see you next time!

check OUT THE STUDENT

QUIT NOW

Once you pass, you'll be much older and more experienced, so you'll be a very safe and responsible motorist. Congratulations! Now let's put that cone-flattening skill to some good use!

what DAT

OK 2 RETAKE LATER

PICK YOUR RIDE!

OH, RIDE! NEED A LIFT?

OBVS

Now that you've passed the driver's test at the DUV, it's time to pick your vehicle. The Uglyverse is filled with one-of-a-kind vehicles, all customized to meet the needs of the driver. Sometimes the driver needs to be taken off the road. So not those needs.

I PASSED MY DRIVER'S TEST!

JUST BARELY

They gave me this.

Let's take a tour of the many different vehicles of the Uglyverse. From Ugly town cars to the cars of Uglytown, you'll find the car that's right for you in no time. And if you're into boats, you've come to the right place! Old boats aplenty round these parts!

PONY RIDE
2000

BABO'S COOKIE CRUISER

TREADING-WATER
CAPRIS

OLD JALOPY

Babo was watching TV this one time, for some reason, and the used-car-lot commercial said: "Trade in your old boat and we'll throw in a free bag of cookies!" Well, Babo knew right away what he had to do . . . get an old boat! What a deal! Wait, but only a captain can own a boat. So Babo set out to get his sea legs. Wait, but a boat needs water to go! So many steps! The cookie trade-in deal started to sound like a scam.

Now Babo drives the all-land, some-sea S.S. Uh-oh. It has power steering and a power anchor!

Babo sails the seventeen seas in search of a better cookie. This usually takes an hour or so. Then he spends a good three hours pulling up that heavy anchor. The good news is, his S.S. Uh-oh goes from zero to sixty! Eventually.

Ahoy!

WAGE'S BIG TOW

As you may already know, Wage's vehicle of choice is his Big Tow truck. He gets plenty of chances to make use of the exciting tow features. Once a week, in fact! That's how often Babo decides to hit the open road.

Those open roads have since been closed.

Wage is a hard worker. He also likes to help anyone in need of assistance.

what's a toe?

The good news is that hundreds of drivers need assistance on the road every day!

For really tough jobs, Wage brings out the bigger tows.

Bigger TOW

TOW-A-TOWN ROBO TOW

GET UGLY REST STOP

PLease Give it a Rest.

Maybe they sell wheels!

You can't drive all day without taking breaks! When you're taking long road trips, we recommend stopping at the Take-a-Break Ugly rest stop. Give your arms a rest and let your wallet do the driving for a while!

TAKE-A- BREAK PAD

Chips! DRINKS! BATHRooms! HAUNTED Dungeon!

You can't drive when you have to go to the bathroom! And you can't go to the bathroom unless you wait in line all day! So plan ahead! The Take-a-Break center has a state-of-the-art restroom system, allowing you to browse through the selection of scented navigational goods.

Propeller
PANTS

GAG-GIFT
SNORKEL

10-GALLON
ALTERNATE-DIMENSION
DOORWAY HAT

SUPER-ITCHY
BLANKET

FLOCKED
BOBHEAD
DOG

CAR-
THEFT
SPRAY

MUD
FLAPS

5-GALLON
ORANGE
"DRINK"

Plunko's car wash is a must! The open road can be a pretty dusty, dirty ordeal for your car. Super-bonus extras include toothbrushes for motorcyclists, a hairbrush for puppy, and a small rag for self-drying.

RACE
TO THE END

Speaking of things that go, nothing's faster than a race car tuned to perfection here in the Uglyverse.

The Good ole UGLY DAYS
of way back when

So did Uglytown always have bad traffic and loud radios? Yes! But back then, cars didn't go as fast.

Long ago, vehicles were pulled by living creatures! This was before the invention of the rear-wheel drive. Now the living things push!

Even bicycles were old! Ah, but those were simple times!

Most vehicles in those days had far less powerful engines. And the Uglys were far more patient.

They still had to watch out for running the red lights, though.

Uglytown Fire Tours are back! Citizens of Uglytown can now get an aerial view of close calls and heroic rescues.

Who doesn't feel that special something when a fire truck saves their home from certain doom? Now you can follow fire trucks from emergency to emergency! No more stiff neck!

If fire isn't your thing, stay far away from the E-K-G food cart! Spicy, spicy!

If you like police cars, the Uglyverse is the universe for you! The Uglys have some of the slickest enforcement vehicles ever!

Yes, that's a giant robot! Who would even think of robbing a bank with this guy roaming the streets! Wedgehead and Ox? Hmm, true. Well, for them we have the brand-new False Getaway Car! Pretty smarty, eh?

FALSE GETAWAY
CAR

CONSTRUCTION
& TOUGH SKATEBOARDS!

Some things that go help us build the things that don't go anywhere at all.

It's FUN TO stay at the...

Cookie STORE?

Wage and Babo spend a lot of their free time on skateboards. With the new backhoe skateboards, nobody can say you aren't getting any work done!

These special dirt-moving vehicles help move mud and grime from your yard to the neighbor's yard! They help build houses too.

DIRT-ON-U

This dump truck is going to dump a
brand-new home on someone's yard!
Hopefully, they cleared the old one
away.

DEER UGLY'S FOREST RANGER VAN

Deer Ugly drives his Antleromeo through the Ugly Woods every night to make sure the ugly little animals are OK. Ok and far away from HIM! Scary! What if there is such a thing as bears? Ooooh! Anyway, his horn brings comfort as he drives along in the night. Beep beep . . . or is it <u>help</u> <u>help</u>?

YOU ARE HERE

The reality of the situation . . .

HEAVYWEIGHT CHAMPION SEAT BELT

EYE ON THE OTHER ROAD

HANDS ALMOST REACH, KINDA

NEED A LIFT?

FEET CAN'T TOUCH

Deer Ugly's ranger gift shop has everything you need to enjoy the great outdoors.

Just don't forget to cover the Antleromeo up at night.
Beep beep.

Do you have gas? No? Neither does the local PAY 'N' PAY gas station!

All automobiles in Uglytown run on electricity! If you need a recharge, pull right up to any PAY 'N' PAY, then pay . . . and pay some more.

Bingo! You're all set!

Dirty windows? No kidding! No worries, though.
The staff doesn't mind!

It's true! In the old days they used to power
cars with oil! Cod-liver oil, castor oil . . . .
all kinds!

Now the Uglys
use Uglyworm
power! Go,
Uglyworm, go!

UGLY CUSTOMS

BORING OLD CAR + CUSTOM PARTS = RAD MOBILE!!!

Everyone in the Uglyverse LOVES to customize their cars, boats, and bikes. Customization makes your vehicle YOUR vehicle . . . there's no mistaking it for anyone else's. Your car should radiate your own personality. This also makes stolen cars easier to find.

Simply describe how many windows, chimneys (if any), ski lifts, conveyor belts, movie screens . . . just go down the list.

BEFORE

AFTER

Customs? No! CUSTOMS! As in personalization! No, not COSTUMES! That's in book 1.

BEFORE

AFTER

The Uglys customize the inside too!

Some more than others.

When the hardworking citizens of Uglytown need to unwind, they go home and sleep. That's when the less careful folks get out the hot air and RACE!

There are no winners, so you don't have to worry about looking like a loser.

ABIMA'S CHOP SHOP

AUTO-REPAIR GARAGE & MAGIC SHOW

HE CHOPS PRICES

...DOWN TO JUST KIND OF HIGH.

Abima runs the best auto-repair shop in town. Brand-new used car broke down? Key snapped off in the ignition? Uglydog on a treadmill not working out for you?

I GOT TIRED.

Blah! Easy stuff! Abima can fix anything. Even sporting events!

Abima has a special facility where he can repair anything. Just look at the junk lying around! Junk lying around is a sign of pure genius! Did you know that? Well, that's why they call this a guide and not a book of stuff you knew already.

I JUST WAVE MY MAGIC WAND!!!

This seems FAMILIAR... watch your wallet!

RIDE THE
UGLYWAY
GET RAILROADED!

ALL ABOARD!

yes, But at what PRICE!?

The Uglyway subway helps move everyone from here to there. It does all of this underground! That way the folks driving cars aboveground don't feel silly.

STATE-of-the-ART stain-proof design!

which stains ARE REAL?!

All of the Ugly subway cars have been refitted with all-new stainproof seats! There are stains but you have no proof!

Some seats offer fake stains so you can hold your spot.

WHAT!?

The Ugly subway is always safe. Because the citizens of Uglytown are so kind and courteous, you never have to worry about getting lost or into any trouble. Of course, if you listen to Uglyworms, that's your problem and there's not much we can do for you there.

Because of overcrowding, the Uglyway engineers have decided to build up! And up and up! This makes for great head room. Things could get tricky in tunnels, but we'll cross that bridge when we have enough bridge-crossing money. The lines are nice and long! That way you can put off your train ride until later.

The Neighborhood DRIVE-IN DRIVE-THRU & SNACK CENTER

On hot summer nights, nothing beats the heat like a night at the drive-in! Not only do they play your favorite channels, they record while you watch in case you missed something on your way back to the snack bar.

ADMIT IT

TICKETS

NOW PLAYING
channel 3

As you can see, going to the drive-in promotes family togetherness and teenage macho moves!

SNACK CHECKLIST

NEXT-CAR SNACK GRAB ☐

BAD MOVIE B-GONE ☐

MOSTLY WATER ☐

Cheap CHIPS ☐

EXPENSIVE DIP ☐

TAKO CONE ☐

CHICKEN A LA KING

Book on Tape ☐

A good Book ☐

CONVERTIBLE SPECIAL ☐

If snacks are a staple in Uglytown, the drive-in snack bar is the whole stapler. You can't beat our snacks! But you can eat them! Most of the time.

But please don't bring your own remote control from home. Customers become confused when the channel changes without warning.

BURGER WATER
DRIVE THRU
& ESCAPE POD!!!

Cinko HATES water! So what if his entire family orders water at the drive-thru? No problem!

Cinko's latest ride comes equipped with an escape pod!! Burger Water has been offering escape pods to all families who qualify.

To qualify, you must promise to eat at Burger Water again.

Have you noticed? Pop singers and drive-thru-window attendants use the same headphones!

What would driving be without somewhere to drive through? Drive-thru windows are more important to cars than tires! Less important than tires filled with air, though.

There's nothing better than eating on the road! Well, when you don't have time to visit the drive-thru, you can visit the drive-by! Eat & Go restaurants on wheels make meals lots of fun and keep you moving constantly! Good for digestion? No, but who has time for digesting these days?

The On-the-Side Car side-dish express is the express way to happiness. The slow route is on the next page.

Poe's Risky Pizza delivers more often than other places that don't deliver at all. The trick is to deliver every pizza at once.

The Golden Uglyworm is best known for its fragrant selection of multicolored foods. Go for the green stuff! MMMM, good!

MOVE IT!

WEDGEHEAD & OX'S MOVING SERVICE

we Move you TO TEARS!

we also Move Money!

Need to move? Need to move in a hurry? Ox and Wedgehead know how that feels. No worries! They happen to run a pretty Ok moving business: MOVE IT! Just make sure you use really strong tape on your boxes.

THE LOAN ARRANGER!

LENDY SPENDY

ATM

Ox and Wedgehead move all sorts of items!

When you gotta go, you gotta go. Welcome to Ugly Air! Please remember our motto: "You should have gone before we left!"

As you can see, there are several types of
aircraft owned and operated by Ugly Air.
Many of them fly! And as you can't see,
the in-flight movie has been canceled.

All mail in Uglytown gets where it needs to go at lightning-fast speeds!

Ice delivery is a little on the slow side. So sometimes we call it water.

When you really want to get it there in a hurry, try Ox and Wedgehead's Speedy Throw Express! Fast, cheap, and through your window by noon!

And for cookies . . . no, wait, they've mysteriously vanished.

WEDGEHEAD SUPREME

Wedgehead loves
his TV! He also
loves your TV
The Wedgehead
Supreme is the perfect
entertainment vehicle!

Just sit back, relax, and watch ..... for the police!

Fold down to watch
other people's TVs!

Welcome to the submarine races! The first one to make it all the way wins! So basically, there are no winners.

SUBMARINE RACE

BUT I JUST WASHED IT!

SINK OR SWIM 2000

Should the water be on the inside?

SWIM FASTER!

There are four types of submarines in the Uglyverse. Big, expensive ones, sandwich subs, sink-or-swim subs, and row-powered subs. Oh, and sunken subs. So that's five types.

Row, Row, Row MY BOAT!!

HMM? Who's #5?

SCHOOL BUS

& AFTER-SCHOOL Buses

You knew the Uglys had a special school bus.
But did you know about the after-school
buses?

Life in the Uglyverse is a lot like waiting for the bus. It's HOW you wait that matters. To find the truth, look within!
(The truth is, the bus stopped running an hour ago.)